USBORNE BIBLE TALES

Loaves and Fishes

Retold by Heather Amery
Illustrated by Norman Young

Designer: Maria Wheatley
Language consultant: Betty Root
Series editor: Jenny Tyler

This is Jesus.

He lived a long time ago in Palestine. He went to the towns and villages with his twelve disciples.

Jesus talked to the people.

Everywhere he went, people came to listen. He told them about God and how they should pray to him.

One day, Jesus sailed across the lake.

He and his disciples stopped at a quiet place on the shore. They climbed a hill and sat down to rest.

Soon lots of people came.

They heard Jesus was there. They came from the towns and villages until there was a huge crowd.

"Tell them to go home," said a disciple.

Jesus felt very sorry for the people. He talked to them, answered questions and made the ill ones well again.

"Now send them away."

"It's getting late and the people are hungry," said a disciple. "They have no food."

"We must feed them," said Jesus.

"Even a huge amount of money would not buy food for them all," said Philip, one of the disciples.

A small boy stood up.

He opened his bag. "Look, I have brought a picnic with me," he said to Andrew, another disciple.

"This boy has food."

"He has five little bread rolls and two small fishes," Andrew said to Jesus. "Not much for this huge crowd."

"May I take your picnic?"

"Will you share it with us?" Jesus asked the boy.
"Yes, Master," said the boy. "Thank you," said Jesus.

Jesus took the food.

"Tell the people to sit down," Jesus said to the disciples. There were about five thousand people.

Jesus held up the loaves and fishes.

He said a prayer of thanks to God. Then he broke up the food into pieces. "Give it to the people," he said.

The disciples gave out the food.

The people sat down on the grass. The more food
the disciples gave out, the more there seemed to be.

Everyone had enough to eat.

The disciples were very surprised. The five thousand people ate bread and fish until they were full.

Then the people went home.

"Collect up the leftover food," said Jesus. His disciples filled twelve baskets and took them home.